W. E. Windus

Illiam Dhone

A Drama

W. E. Windus

Illiam Dhone
A Drama

ISBN/EAN: 9783337383565

Printed in Europe, USA, Canada, Australia, Japan

Cover: Foto ©Andreas Hilbeck / pixelio.de

More available books at **www.hansebooks.com**

Illiam Dhône:

A DRAMA.

BY

W. E. WINDUS.

1886.

ILLIAM DHÔNE.

ACT I.

Scene. 1.—THE GUARD-ROOM IN PEEL.

Soldiers seated round the fire. *Enter* SOLDIER.

FIRST SOLDIER.
Rouse up the fire, old comrade : by my faith
These Autumn nights are cold.   The dense sea-mist,
As I stood sentinel beneath the tower,
Pierced to the very marrow of my bones.
The Captain has returned ?

SECOND SOLDIER.
Not yet I ween,
Unless he entered by the postern door.

THIRD SOLDIER.
Hast heard the news ?

FIRST SOLDIER.
What news, my beardless boy ?
Some of thy grandam's cackle from the hills ?

THIRD SOLDIER.
Go to, thou knave, and let my grandam be.

FOURTH SOLDIER.
Or she may cast a spell upon thy bones,
That never fire may warm but that of—

Second Soldier.

Hush !—
And, comrades, guard your tongues.   But yester-e'en
Our sergeant plainly heard the Moddey Dhoo
Howling and baying 'neath the chapel walls ;
A sure forewarning of adversity.

Third Soldier.

A murrain on your hound ! I don't believe—

Second Soldier.

Be silent, Dan.   You're but a raw recruit ;
We seasoned soldiers have both seen and heard.
It may be your turn soon ; and, when it come,
Let no foul oath or whisper pass your lips
While in its presence.

Third Soldier

Hast thou seen the thing ?

Second Soldier.

Aye, many a time I've seen its fearful form.
A week before you joined, it entered here,
And stretched its shaggy length upon the floor,
To bask beside the ruddy firelight's glow.
Perchance an hour it lay there, and its eyes
Shone like the red-hot embers of the hearth,
And its white fangs gleamed bright as burnished steel.

Third Soldier.

And then ?

Second Soldier.

It passed as noiseless as it came.
But hark !—I hear the sentry at the gate ;
He challenges.   The captain has returned.
The track from Rushen sure was hard to keep
In this foul fog.—Now, comrade, for your news.

THIRD SOLDIER.

You might have heard it sooner had you willed :
But let it pass. Scarce three short hours ago,
I chanced to bear despatches to the town,
And as I crossed the quay and picked my way,
Among the hawsers of the harboured ships,
I saw Receiver-General —Illiam Dhône—
In earnest confab with another man.
The mist was thick, and so I followed near,
And heard them speak of troublous times abroad ;
How in the Isle adjacent to our own,
That's named Great Britain, bloody wars impend ;
And how a man called " Noll," a brewer's son,
Is bearding Charles upon his very throne.

FIRST SOLDIER.

Well, let him beard him.   What is that to us ?
I'd warrant ye he'd never beard our Earl.

THIRD SOLDIER.

And then they spoke of liberties and rights,
And Illiam prayed a blessing on our Isle,
And on all Manxmen who are staunch and true ;
And then they passed away amid the mist.

SECOND SOLDIER.

And who the other man ?   Didst know him, lad ?

THIRD SOLDIER.

No, I did not.   The only thing I marked
Was that I heard our Illiam call him " Ned."

SECOND SOLDIER.

His brother, boy ; I heard he had returned—
Stern Edward Christian.   What a difference
There is between the two !   Our Illiam Dhône
Is like the sunlight on a summer sea,
But Edward is a black-browed thunder-cloud.

THIRD SOLDIER.

He minded me of one of those sleek priests
Who suck like slugs the fatness of the soil;
And, as I oft have heard my grandam say,
There's much lost 'twixt the fingers and the mouth,
When they are near.

FOURTH SOLDIER.

Thy grandam !—That old witch ?
She'd even black the babe within the womb
With her foul tongue.

THIRD SOLDIER.

Her tongue speaks always truth.
But truth is foul to those who live by lies.

FOURTH SOLDIER.

Well, have thy say.   It matters not to me.

THIRD SOLDIER.

But much to others.   I'll not hear ill words
Of one who reared me, orphan from my birth.
Witch or no witch, she never injured thee,
Nor ever wove a spell against a foe;
But being wiser than the folk around,
And skilled in herbal lore and simple charms,
They over-look the good she does for them,
In search for evil.   Should the fiend himself
Rise up from Hell against her, I would hurl—

SECOND SOLDIER.

Beshrew thy tongue !   See there !   The Moddey Dhoo !

Scene 2.—RONALDSWAY.

MISTRESS CHRISTIAN.

Ah me!   How wearily the hours roll by,
Mist on the mountains, mist upon the sea,

And all the sky a heavy ashen pall!
Surely, Mannanan's spirit haunts the Isle.
How it depresses me! With every breath
I seem to draw a sorrow to my soul;
But most I mourn my husband's clouded brow,
My fair-haired Illiam, who was once so gay,
Whose every glance was like a sunny ray;
But now his looks alarm me. Would I knew
The secret grief that rankles in his breast.
Held in high honour by our Lord the Earl,
Loved through the Island both by rich and poor,
Whence comes his care? Alas! I cannot tell,
Nor would I weary him with questioning.
I must be loyal, not inquisitive,
For he is ever loyal unto me;
And soon, may be, he'll take me to his heart,
And tell me of his trouble; and I'll draw
The cankering venom seething in the wound,
And soothe him of his sorrow. Ah! my love—
But hark! I hear a footstep.—It is he.

[*Enter* WILLIAM CHRISTIAN *and* EDWARD.]

WILLIAM CHRISTIAN.

What, all alone, my dear one, and in tears?
I have been truant long; but Edward, here,
Will tell you on what urgent errand bent.

EDWARD CHRISTIAN.

Greeting, sweet sister. I but yesterday
Arrived from England, leaving trouble there,
To find more trouble even on our Isle.
For Illiam, meeting me last eve at Peel,
Told me a tale of angry discontent
Among the holders of the lands of Mann,
To match the news I brought from England's shore,
Where Revolution holds the Throne at bay.

And all this day we've spurred through mist and mire,
From Peel to South Barrule and Douglas Bay,
To hear but piteous plaints of grievous wrong,
And cries against oppression ; and indeed
I thought our Illiam's tender heart would burst
With indignation—seeing no redress.

MISTRESS CHRISTIAN.

Pardon me, Edward, for my want of thought.
So travel-stained and weary,—Illiam, too,
A cup of wine will cheer your drooping hearts ;
So leave me for awhile, and join me here
When you have found refreshment.

[*Exeunt* W. *and* E. CHRISTIAN.]

MISTRESS CHRISTIAN.
Ah ! at last
I hold the clue to my poor Illiam's mood.
I might have guessed 'twas care for those he loves,
For all his heart is centred in our Isle
And in its people. Well may he be loved,
For he is all for them and for their rights,
And would uphold them even to the death.
And yet I cannot bear to see him brooa—
It may be selfish—on their petty wrongs ;
For he to me is as they are to him,
Nay, dearer, for my soul itself is his ;
But still my pride, at warfare with my love,
Makes me rejoice that they should hold his heart.
Ah ! what a pure unselfish life is his !
Sharing their sorrows, joying in their joys,
He passes through the Island like a saint,
Crowned with the halo of a people's love.
Would that my woman's wit might frame some scheme
To aid him in his labour—bring redress ;
That laggard Justice, hovering high in air,

Might, like a wide-winged falcon of Glen Meay,
Swoop down upon the raven's ravenous brood,
And rid our Island of iniquity!

WILLIAM CHRISTIAN—*enters.*

My brother Edward, fairly spent with toil,
Sends his excuses.   He would rest awhile.
Our hurried ride—his three rough nights at sea,
Have well-nigh over-taxed his iron will,
And I have left him slumbering like a child,

MISTRESS CHRISTIAN.

And may he slumber soundly, Illiam dear!
I hold him safer sleeping than awake ;
For if the whispers of our Isle be true,
He plays a dangerous game on England's shore,
Where his companions are of ill repute,
Adventurers and plotters 'gainst the Throne.
I pray you, Illiam, be not led away
By a too specious tongue—but stand aloof,
And lend not rashly your good name to those
Who would but use it to your detriment.

WILLIAM CHRISTIAN.

Oh! have no fear, fond wife.   Our Mona's wrongs
More than suffice to keep me to the course.
I need no spur of foreign policy
To force me to allegiance—be assured.
I, of the people, hold the peoples' rights,
And will maintain them—Heaven aiding me—
Till we regain our tenure of the straw,
And all our liberties and rightful claims ;
But by fair dealing—not by sorry plots,
Which would but end in ruin to us all.
And yet I know not how to win their cause.
I can but mourn with them in sympathy,
For what avails the weak against the strong?

2

And yet the people's voice is voice of God,
So should prevail.   But ah ! the waiting time.
To hear the mournful clamour of their cries
Wind-borne from mountain-side and green-wood glen,
Impatient words and sullen mutterings,
Like distant thunder rolling through the sky ;—
See eyes that flash with furious impotence,
To smite oppression in its hold of power,
As I have seen the angry lightning strike
Grey-crested Greeba in its garb of gold,
And scatter from its crags and pass away
Amid the mocking echoes of the hills.

MISTRESS CHRISTIAN.

Illiam, but only yester evening
Your old nurse Sheila, sorrowing sore, came here
To tell me of her trouble.   Poor old soul !
Her grandson Dan, to ease her of his keep,
Has joined the ranks of our militia.
'Twas sad to see the piteous look she wore,
So I persuaded her to rest awhile
Beneath our roof-tree.   She is very wise,
And full of counsel—let me bring her here.

[*Exit* MISTRESS CHRISTIAN.   *Re-enter with* SHEILA CRAINE.]

WILLIAM CHRISTIAN.

Welcome, good nurse !   With pleasure I can say
Your grandson makes a mark among our men—
So straight and steady.   Though he left your roof,
His heart is still with you—that well I know ;
But, as he told me, your poor plot of ground—
All eaten up with charges and with tithes—
Is scarcely worth its tillage.   So he thought
It better to enlist.   And I must say
That I admire the manhood of his act.

SHEILA CRAINE.

Yes, Illiam Dhône; and well enough I know
Smaller the company, the more the share.
But I would rather starve upon a crust,
So he have plenty, than fare regally
Without his loving face beside my hearth.
But pass it by—'tis done; I wait your words.
Speak, Illiam Dhône, and tell me of *your* care.

MISTRESS CHRISTIAN.

You know full well, dear Sheila, all his care—
Our poor down-trodden people. What we want
Is how to find a cure for so much care.

SHEILA CRAINE.

It has been written that God laughs with joy
To see a poor man helping poverty.
Would He not frown to see one high in power
Taking no heed but passing by the poor?
Go to the Earl, and bear him all our woes;
And tell him Sheila Craine, of Slieu Chiarne,
Sends him this warning: "After spring-tide—Neap!"
The life-blood now beats high within his veins,
But I have seen, with eyes that look afar,
A headless corpse wrapped in a gory shroud,
And heard the night-wind whisper—"Stanlagh Mooar!

MISTRESS CHRISTIAN.

Oh! Sheila, you affright me. 'Twas a dream!
Our puissant lord laid low?—It could not be!
Yet your advice seems reasonable and fair.
Go, Illiam, to the Earl—he trusts in thee—
And tell him of our troubles. Pray him call
A gathering of the Isle to Tynwald Hill,
To hear our grievances and just complaints.
And may the God who guides us move his heart
To do his devoir by our Isle and thee!

2A

Scene 3.—TYNWALD HILL.—EARL OF DERBY *and* W. CHRISTIAN.
At foot of the hill crowd dispersing.

EARL OF DERBY.

Now, William Christian, art thou satisfied ?
At thy request I called this motley crowd
Of all our vassals.   Every parish sent
Its representatives.   From far Kirk Bride,
And Kirk Malew—Kirk German and Maughold,
Kirk everywhere I ween, and patiently,—
For Manxmen's speech is apt to run apace,—
I waited on the clatter of their tongues,
Stooping from my prerogative to hear.
So I have granted them one boon at least,
The liberty of speech ; and, rest assured,
The angry cloud that threatened has dissolved,
With this assembly, into summer rain.

WILLIAM CHRISTIAN.

But summer rain sometimes, my lord, returns ;
Rising in vapour from the heated earth
To form fresh clouds and burst again in storm.
You granted them full liberty of speech,
Held out fair hope, and soothed their aching hearts
With promises of aid ; and, trusting you,
They have dispersed their several ways in peace.
But after this—I know our Manx folk well—
Unless they have their ancient liberties
And their just rights restored to them in full,
To-day will add fresh fuel to the fire,
Which only smoulders now within their breasts,
To burst again to morrow o'er the Isle,
In conflagration of conspiracy.

EARL OF DERBY.

Thou speakest boldly, Christian.   Were it not
That I have ever proved thee staunch and true,

I might imagine thou wert linked with those
Who breed rebellion.   Surely thou must know,
Without my sanction there is no redress,
Nor even an appeal against my will ; —
That I, as King of Mann, hold every right ?

WILLIAM CHRISTIAN.

Can they be rights gained by cajolery ?
Our simple people yielded up their lands,
Inherited by them in days of yore
From sire to son by tenure of the straw ;
Forced into compromise by legal liars,
Who fatten on foul frauds and lawless laws ;
While Agriculture, blighted, droops and dies,
And gaunt-eyed Famine stalks across the fields.
One king-like right, great Earl, I own you hold—
The right of justice.   Let it shine on those—
Poor simple souls—who pleaded here to-day,
And grant their sighs and sorrows full relief.
A people's grief may never be despised.
A streamlet now it trickles from the hills :
The winter rains may flush it to a flood—
A people's passion, swollen high with tears—
To burst aside all law, and sweep away,
In deluge dire, the land-marks of a realm.
Look now at England !—In what dark distress—
The waves ascending even to the Throne—
And ask thy heart, and ponder on the cause :
A People's voice against a weak King's will.
Look there and learn, my lord, and pardon me,
If my plain speaking mars my courtesy.

EARL OF DERBY.

Christian, I know full well thy honest heart
Means no offence against my sovereignty.
I only grieve to see thee more incline
To Puritans and such rebellious hounds,

Than to King Charles' loyal Cavaliers ;
For all my heart is with my brother King,
And I would fain see thee arrayed with us,
To crush down Cromwell and his canting crew,
Holding the King's commission with your sword.
That, Christian, rests with thee. Now for the cause--
Which thou hast pleaded well, I must allow—
The restitution to our tenantry
Of all the liberties they held of yore.
There's reason, too, in some of their demands ;
And, as I promised them, I now maintain
That they shall meet due justice at my hands ;—
But by and bye, Receiver ; by and bye.
I cannot alter everything at once,
Nor yet accede to every favour asked :
These troublous times are apt to bring contempt
On rulers too light-handed in their rule ;
For we must hold our people in its place,
Nor let it step too near our sacred thrones.
They shall have justice if they wait awhile,
And be more patient and amenable.

WILLIAM CHRISTIAN.
But while they wait, my lord, the children starve—

EARL OF DERBY.
And, if they starve, 'twill be their parents' fault.
Tell them to till their lands, not waste their time
In idle arguments and vain disputes.
Leave me to right the wrong where it exists—
But at my leisure not at their command ;
Or they shall feel that I *am* King in Mann.

Scene 4.—IN THE COURT YARD. CASTLE RUSHEN.

FIRST SOLDIER.

'Tis as I said, lads. Our great Earl departs
This eve for England ; and the vessel waits
To bear him o'er the sea to help Prince Charles.

SECOND SOLDIER.

I hear a man named Cromwell rules the land,
Smiting alike with Bible and with sword.

THIRD SOLDIER.

And the poor King beheaded ?—

FIRST SOLDIER.

So they say.
This morning Illiam Dhône spurred here in haste,—
I knew him by his coat of Lincoln green—
Leapt from the saddle, hurried through the gate—

FOURTH SOLDIER.

And now is with the Earl. Young Patrick Kneen
Carried despatches ere the day had dawned
To Ronaldsway, and has not long returned.

THIRD SOLDIER.

Our Illiam's high in favour with the Earl !

FOURTH SOLDIER.

More so than with the Countess, I've been told.

FIRST SOLDIER.

Maybe he will accompany the Earl
To distant England, there to judge the man
Who slew the King to sit upon his throne ?

SECOND SOLDIER.

Sit on his throne? God's truth! He pulled it down,
And with its fragments lighted such a fire
That all the Isle of Britain is aflame!

THIRD SOLDIER.

Then I suppose they'll bring the scoundrel here,
And try him for his crime on Tynwald Hill?
But hark!—The bugle sounding for parade.

[*Enter* EARL *and* COUNTESS *with* W. CHRISTIAN.]

EARL OF DERBY *to* COUNTESS.

As I have said, I know no trustier man
Than William Christian. I should be ashamed
In such a noble cause to show delay,
And let my fingers loiter on the hilt
While my good sword is leaping from its sheath :
And so, fair Queen, I leave thee—not alone,
But in the care of one who loves us well ;
One who would hold our Island with his life,
And with our Island its beloved Queen.

WILLIAM CHRISTIAN.

I thank thee, sire ; and I accept this trust
To honour it as far as in me lies.

EARL OF DERBY.

Then, Christian, I can go so far content ;
And I appoint you colonel of our troops,
And commandant of all our fortresses.
Nay—not a word. I know the power you hold
Upon our people. Now I give thee power
To use such hold with due authority.

COUNTESS OF DERBY.

I well approve the choice, my lord, you make ;
Knowing how able he has ever been

To lead our Manxmen, even with a word.
I sometimes think our subjects look to him
More as their ruler even than their lord.

WILLIAM CHRISTIAN.

Madam, the simple influence I hold
Among our people lies within their hearts :
A loving power obtained by gentle words,
And homely offices among the poor.
The Earl departs—for how long no one knows—
This eve for England, leaving me in charge
Not only of his realm, but his fair name ;
A trust of high responsibility.
Aid me in asking, madam, ere he go,
That he will grant the people peace at last
By restitution of their ancient rights,
He promised them—aye, many months ago,—
To help them to redress and liberty ;
And patiently they've waited on his word.
Now they will say : ' Our Lord has gone away
To fight for foreign causes, leaving ours
Unheeded and disdained ! '—And should they rise——

COUNTESS OF DERBY.

Pest on the people ! Should the people rise
Means are at hand to put them down again.
And should you falter, through false clemency,
I would myself ride out and head our troops,
And lead them through their ranks, and break them down
Low as the whirlwind lays the autumn grain.

EARL OF DERBY.

Well spoken, Countess!—Brave as you are fair !
Our Christian's heart is made of softer stuff ;
But he will do his duty honestly.
This disaffection that he harps upon
Is past and gone to all the winds that blow.

Soon ripe, soon rotten, Manx conspiracies,
As I well know—he better perhaps than I—
For every Manxman leans upon his lips,
And he can lead the people as he will.

WILLIAM CHRISTIAN.
I cannot, on such terms, accept command.
To do my duty to the Isle and thee,
God helping me, will always be my care.
But rather, Sire, than lift my arm to smite
The people that I love, I'd hew it off,
And think its loss a gain. Rather than use
My tongue in specious argument for wrong,
I'd pluck it from my throat and cast it down
Before the dogs, and be for ever dumb.

COUNTESS OF DERBY.
Better that you had never owned a tongue
Than it should give your thoughts such utterance.
My ears are burning now with very shame,
Defiled by hearing such disloyal words.

EARL OF DERBY.
Nay, Countess, chide him not. He speaks but truth,
And I respect the boldness of his words;
And knowing what he means, I'd rather trust
My honour to his care than to some knave
Who, truckling to my face, behind my back
Would stab me with some subtle treachery.
Whate'er he say, I know that in his heart
He is a true and loyal Cavalier.

COUNTESS OF DERBY—*aside.*
A Cavalier! A puling Puritan!

EARL OF DERBY.
So, Christian, no denial. You shall hold
The Island in our absence and shall act

In everything according to your will,
So far as martial rule and discipline ;
In other things relating to our state,
Acting but on approval of the Queen.
Nay—no more words—I mean to be obeyed,
For I have much to settle and arrange,
And Time, the rebel, will not wait for Kings.
As for the people, they *must* wait awhile ;
But when we've cut these canting Roundheads down,
And set Prince Charlie firm upon his throne,
Then we will hold high revel in our Isle,
And grant the people all that they desire.
I can do nothing now.   But this I swear :
If they keep faith with me, I will with them—
When I return.—Fair Christian, fare thee well !

ACT II.

Scene 1.—CASTLE TOWN.

MISTRESS CHRISTIAN.

Ask me not, Illiam, to break this news.
I dare not tell her—'tis too terrible.
For in the fiery depths of her despair
The Countess loses all her womanhood.
When I approached her but a week ago,
She met me with clenched teeth and flashing eyes,
Tearless and dry, the while her bosom heaved
As though 'twould burst the bodice of her robe.
No sob or sigh escaped her ashen lips ;
But, like a tigress wounded to the death,
She lashed herself to fury as I stood
Speechless before her, trembling in my tears.

WILLIAM CHRISTIAN.

Too stern the task, I fear, my gentle wife,
For she despises woman's tenderness.
I mind me of the morning when I bore
News of the execution of the Earl.
She gave one sob—sprang forward from her couch,
And stood before me stricken into stone.
No grief—no rage. She merely raised her hand,
And pointed to the door ; and I retired,
Awed by the awful silence of her grief.
And yet she must be told, and told at once,
That insurrection rages in the Isle.
I thought perchance a woman's gentle voice
Might better soothe the ill she has to bear,
So laid a task on you which should be mine.
Now I must see her, take it as she will :
I can no longer hold the people back :

From every quarter they are hurrying here,
First in a whisper 'Stanlagh Mooar is dead'
Spread like a fire upon a gorse-clad hill;
Then with a clarion cry the whole Isle rang:
'Now we will seize upon our own again.'

SHEILA CRAINE—*enters*.

Through the long night I've hurried on my way
To warn you that at last the hour is come,
To strike for justice and fair liberty.
The people's cry is swelling in the air;
The burden of that cry is 'Illiam Dhône:
The people's Friend shall be the people's King.
We call on him to heal our festering wounds;
We look to him to lead us to our rights!'
Go, Illiam Dhône, and meet them as their King.

MISTRESS CHRISTIAN.

No, Sheila, no! He could not act such part.
Think of the promise that he gave the Earl,
To guard the Countess even with his life.
He dare not, would not, break his plighted word;
And, now the Earl is dead, the more the need
To cherish and protect her.—Illiam, go
And tell the Countess all the bitter truth;
And pray her grant the people their desire
And so stem back the tide and still the waves
Which soon would roar around her.—Illiam, go.

SHEILA CRAINE.

I watched the day break as I wandered here—
A pallid silvern streak above the sea,
And heard the grey-winged sea-mews' mournful cries,
In flight from sea to shore. The light increased
Till all the air was bathed in ruby gleams,
And ebon black, against the blood-red sky,
The sea-mews changed to ravens as I gazed.

Then like a burnished bowl the great sun rose,
And what had seemed black wings were swelling sails
Of mighty ships which speeded from afar,
And all their prows were pointing to our Isle.
I saw their pennons—heard thè cries of men—
And then the vision vanished from my sight,
In purple clouds that gathered on the sea.
Strike, Illiam Dhône, before those clouds draw near,
And make yourself the master of the Isle.

MISTRESS CHRISTIAN.

See yonder, Illiam, see! The Countess comes,
Her sable robe a shadow in the sun.
Go, speak at once, and tell her all we know,
Sparing her pride the blow it would receive
Should this fresh trouble strike her unprepared.

EDWARD CHRISTIAN—*enters hurriedly.*

Within an hour a grim and gaunt array
Of famished tenants of the lands of Mann
Will gather howling at the Castle gates.
I spurred my jaded steed before their hosts
To tell you, Illiam, that with every mouth
You are proclaimed their leader and their King.

COUNTESS OF DERBY—*approaching slowly.*

What means this rumour, Master Christian—
The people in revolt against our rule?
If there be any truth in such report—
I merely heard it whispered by my maid;
Some idle tattle maybe of the town—
Send out our troops to scour the country round,
And nip rebellion in the very bud.

WILLIAM CHRISTIAN.

Madam, 'tis but too true. My brother passed
A strong detachment marching on the town
Scarcely an hour ago.

COUNTESS OF DERBY.
And you wait here?
Lose not a moment. Call our troops to arms—
And slay these rebels ere they meet my sight.
Give them no quarter; shoot them; cut them down

WILLIAM CHRISTIAN.
Madam, our soldiers' hearts are with their kin,
Bound by the ties of blood they could not shed
Without dishonour. They would never strike
Against their country-men a single blow,
Nor could I take command in such a cause.

COUNTESS OF DERBY.
Traitor! I feel thou art in league with them!

WILLIAM CHRISTIAN.
No traitor, madam, but an honest man,
Ready to guard your honour with his life,
But not by riding down the starving poor.
Besides, the Earl had promised long ago
To grant what I now beg on bended knee;
The restitution of the people's rights.
Delay no longer, madam; let me ride,
Bearing a gracious message—not a sword—
And they will throw themselves before your feet,
And bless you for the boon—and pass away.
Defy them; and I know not what may hap.
I can do nothing more except to die,
Guarding your honour to the very last.

COUNTESS OF DERBY.
I will not act so cowardly a part,
But will defy these rebels to the death.

MISTRESS CHRISTIAN.
Madam, for God's high mercy grant their rights.

COUNTESS OF DERBY.

I will not grant them what they call their rights.
Where be their rights when everything is mine?
Rather than parley with them I will die.

SHEILA CRANE.

Then die, proud Countess, for your doom draws nigh.
I hear the people's murmur in mine ears,
A sound of angry bees from pillaged hives:
I hear the tramp of firm determined feet,
That clank with steel and iron as they come.

EDWARD CHRISTIAN.

Madam, I pray thee yield to their demands—
They only ask their due—and place your name
Upon this parchment which I hold in hand;
And let my brother bear it ere they come.

COUNTESS OF DERBY.

A plot!—I see it now—prepared by you
To meet this rising. No—I will not sign.

MISTRESS CHRISTIAN.

They come—they come.—Oh! madam, yield, I pray,
And save yourself from death or infamy.

WILLIAM CHRISTIAN.

Unless you sign, your kingdom melts away
Like snow in summer. Let me go, I pray,
And stay the torrent which is drawing near
To whelm us all beneath its angry waves.
Sign, madam, sign—the mob is close at hand.

COUNTESS OF DERBY.

Perforce, then, I must yield. Give me the pen:
But this I swear—I only bide my time;
And, when it come, then look for my revenge.
Here—take this thing—accursed document!—

'That you have wrested from a widowed Queen
Who never will forget it or forgive.

SHEILA CRAINE.

Now thou canst ride to meet them as their King;
A King whose throne is in his subjects' hearts.
Bearing their freedom on thy good sword's point,
Ride forth to meet thy people—Illiam Dhône!

Scene 2.—RAMSAY BAY. ENGLISH FLEET AT ANCHOR.

COLONEL DUCKENFIELD.

Where is this Christian? Is the man a myth?
Art sure he had my message? Answer, man.
The day wanes fast, and yet he is not here.

KELLY.

When your tall ships arrived at Douglas Bay,
And signalled to the shore to speak with us,
I manned a boat at once and put to sea;
And, when we gained your side, you picked me out
From all my mates to come to you on board;
Seeing, no doubt, in me a trusty man,
Ready for any service when required.

COLONEL DUCKENFIELD.

Because I heard you speak our English tongue,
That is the reason why I brought you here;
To be of use in rendering my commands
Into the jargon of these Islanders.

KELLY.

And then you sent me back again to shore,
To bear a message to our Illiam Dhône.

COLONEL DUCKENFIELD.

Your Illiam Dhône!—To Colonel Christian, man.
Speak to the purpose—tell me his reply.

4

KELLY.

Soon as our boat touched shore I spoke to him,
And gave your message. I stood by his side,
And heard him order trusty messengers
To ride at once with speed to Castle-town.

COLONEL DUCKENFIELD.

To give the Countess warning, I suppose?

KELLY.

It might be so. I heard not all he said,
For, putting me aside, he passed away.

COLONEL DUCKENFIELD.

But speak, and to the purpose, if you can:
What was the answer Colonel Christian sent?

KELLY.

Although I'm but a simple fisherman,
Drawing my hard-earned wages from the sea
In stormy weather, like our black-backed gulls—

COLONEL DUCKENFIELD.

Confusion seize you and your black-backed gulls!
I want a simple answer. Tell me straight,
What were the words that Colonel Christian used?

KELLY.

Have patience, sir, for what I meant to say
Is that, when wintry winds have roughed the sea,
I do odd jobs among our husbandmen;
And know the Island well from sea to sea.

COLONEL DUCKENFIELD—*aside.*

Confound the man!

KELLY.

And, had you given the word,
I would have watched him till he met you here.

COLONEL DUCKENFIELD.

I want no spies. I only wish to know
The very words that Colonel Christian used.
There may be some mistake. I named this day—

KELLY.

In my opinion—

COLONEL DUCKENFIELD.

Curse your cackling tongue.
Here, corporal, hold this fellow in arrest,
Until he answer plainly what I ask.

KELLY.

Oh! pardon, gracious sir. His words were these :
' Tell him that I will be, to-morrow eve,
At Ramsay Bay before the moon arise ! '

COLONEL DUCKENFIELD.

Ah! that is to the point : but see you there
A single horseman spurring at full speed ?—
He turns this way—and now he gains the town—
Now he dismounts and leaves his smoking steed.
Is that the man ?

KELLY.

Great sir, that is the man.

[W. CHRISTIAN *enters*.]

COLONEL DUCKENFIELD.

So, Colonel Christian, we meet at last.
It would have saved some trouble had you deigned
To meet me when I touched at Douglas Bay,
To hear the orders of the Parliament,
Instead of riding off discourteously.
I hear you hold this island in your hands?

KELLY.

Yes ; Illiam Dhône. This gentleman and I
Were greatly—

4A

Colonel Duckenfield.

Silence, sir—and, corporal,
Take this loquacious fellow to the shore,
And fill his mouth with sea-weed and salt sand,
With anything, in fact, to stay his tongue.
Excuse me, Colonel; but that prating fool
Has buzzed about me all the live-long day,
And stung me into fury, like a gnat.

William Christian.

No fool is Kelly, but a thorough knave.
You might have chosen better, sir, I think.
Now, Colonel Duckenfield, I wait your will.

Colonel Duckenfield.

To you, then, Colonel William Christian,
Receiver-General of the Isle of Mann,
I bear these orders from the Parliament :
That you submit yourself and all your troops,
Together with your fortresses and stores,
Into my hands at once without demur :
Also that you deliver to my charge
Earl Derby's widowed Countess, who is styled
By the inhabitants the Queen of Mann :
Also that you assist me with your troops
In quelling insurrection on the Isle :
If on these points you readily agree,
To entertain and serve the Commonwealth,
That you shall hold all office as before :
If you refuse seditiously these terms,
That I attach your person, and reduce
At once, by fire and sword, this Isle of Mann.

William Christian.

It would be useless, Colonel Duckenfield,
To stand in arms against great Cromwell's power.
Rather than see red bloodshed on our Isle,
I would submit without the least demur.

As for the insurrection, it has passed ;
The people made but clamour for their own,
And forced the Countess to restore their rights.
But two conditions I must ask from you.
First, that the people shall retain their rights ;
And second, that you treat the Countess well
And courteously—remembering how sore
Her trouble lies upon her.   Grant these points,
And I subject myself to your command ;
Refuse—and I, who know our Manx folk well,
Will lead them to resistance till I die.

COLONEL DUCKENFIELD.

Gladly I find that we can come to terms.
I hold authority that all their rights
Be vested in the people as of old.
As for the Countess, if she will consent
To rest in quiet, she can live her life
In freedom on the Isle.   The Earl's estates,
Sequestrated, she cannot now enjoy :
But, if she act with malice, my commands
Are that I hold her actions in restraint.

WILLIAM CHRISTIAN.

Upon these terms I can submit at once ;
And, for the present bidding you farewell,
Will hasten back to Rushen, and prepare
The Countess—if I can—to bear this blow
With patience.   When you will—at any hour,
On Tynwald Hill, with due formality,
I will deliver up the Isle of Mann
Into the keeping of the Parliament ;
Relying on your honour as a man,
Soldier, and gentleman, that you will treat
The widowed Countess with due courtesy ;
And that our peaceful people shall retain
The rights and liberties they held of yore.

Scene 3.—RONALDSWAY.

MISTRESS CHRISTIAN.

How happy am I once again at home !—
The dear old home my husband loves so well—
The sweet scent of the gorse ; the free fresh air,
Filled with the trilling notes of soaring birds,
And mellow murmurings of toiling bees.
How better are our simple pleasures here
Than all the hollow pomps and pride of power.
For Illiam never pushed himself for place ;
But when Lord Fairfax pressed him to accept
The onerous offices of Governor,
He could not well refuse, though well I know
His heart was never anxious for such charge.
The heavy cares of office weigh him down ;
And then he grieves about our hapless Queen,
Holding the key which opes her prison door,
Yet not allowed to turn it in the lock
Which bars her freedom. She, implacable,
Treats him with high disdain, believing him
To be her foe instead of her best friend ;
Or, in her angry mood, upbraiding him
With fiery scorn whene'er he meets her sight.
And then again, that wily Challoner—
I know he envies Illiam his command :
'Tis written in his face. Whene'er he speaks
I mark his heavy eyelids droop and fall,
As I have seen a reptile's, when it meets
The honest sunlight.—Ah ! But who comes here ?

EDWARD CHRISTIAN—*enters.*

'Tis I, sweet sister—Edward Christian,
On matter of much moment. Where is he—
My brother Illiam ? Not away, I trust ?—

MISTRESS CHRISTIAN.

I left him on the terrace by the sea,
Not half an hour ago.

EDWARD CHRISTIAN.
Then send for him—
I pray of you—at once ; and let him know,
I come on business of emergency.

MISTRESS CHRISTIAN.
But, Edward, what is this ?   Your face is pale ;
Your hand is trembling like an aspen leaf.

EDWARD CHRISTIAN.
Nothing but what a stoup of generous wine
Will soon restore.—Ah ! Here he comes at last.

WILLIAM CHRISTIAN—*enters.*
Edward !—The very man I wished to see.
You rode from Peel ?

EDWARD CHRISTIAN.
Aye, Illiam, in haste ;
And, sad to say, I bring you sorry news.
You know the rumours that have spread abroad
Of defalcations in the Treasury ?
Now Challoner, our Chief Commissioner,
Has laid the blame on you.

WILLIAM CHRISTIAN.
The blame on me ?
The crafty knave ! I know how he has worked,
Mole-like, to undermine me.   So at last
He comes upon the surface ?   Let him come.
The fault rests not with me, but more with those
Whom I have trusted, plotters like himself,
And, maybe, in his pay, to ruin me.
The matter shall be sounded to the dregs,
Until this falsehood shall be brought to light.

MISTRESS CHRISTIAN.
But all who know you trust you, Illiam, dear.

EDWARD CHRISTIAN.

Yes, all who know him.   But, I grieve to say,
Some envious men who hold a petty power
Would drag him to the dirt to raise themselves.   ·
This Challoner is one ; and much I fear
He has succeeded.   You must know the worst :—
This very morn a warrant of arrest—

MISTRESS CHRISTIAN.

No, Edward, no !—You only speak in jest ?

EDWARD CHRISTIAN.

'Tis but too true—and he must fly at once :
I see no other course.   If he delay
He falls into their toils a helpless prey ;
But, being free, he will have time to act.

WILLIAM CHRISTIAN.

What ?—Fly, a coward, from such paltry knaves ?
'Twould seem like guilt.

EDWARD CHRISTIAN.

            I tell you you must fly.

MISTRESS CHRISTIAN.

Why, every Manxman would be up in arms,
Remembering how he battled for their rights.

EDWARD CHRISTIAN.

Ah ! sister, you forget that in those days
Our people were half famished, trodden down
Beneath the feet of those who fed on them ;—
Had everything to gain and naught to lose.
But now grown sleek and fat as well-fed steers,
With all their rights confirmed, they would not care
To run the risk of losing them again.
You understand your Manxmen ; I—the world

MISTRESS CHRISTIAN.
But how to save him, Edward?

EDWARD CHRISTIAN.
All's prepared.
As I rode here, I noticed near the gate
That hang-dog rascal, Kelly, waiting here;
To play no doubt the scurvy part of spy.
I'll lead the caitiff such a devil's dance
He little dreams of.   Listen to my plans :
The nights are moonless, happily for us ;
And, when the glooming's fading in the west,
I, having donned our Illiam's uniform,
Will mount and slowly ride upon my way,
While he, in my more sombre garb of grey,
Shall creep among the brackens to the shore ;
Where, off the rock which arches from the cliff,
A boat will be in waiting, with a crew—
No doubt engaged in fishing—trusty men,
Who'll row him to my vessel, standing by
About a mile or little more to sea.
They'll keep good watch : but, should the night be dark,
A little powder flashed within the pan
Of this small pistol will assist their eyes ;
And, when the vessel's gained, he'll make his way
At once to England—there to wait events—
Trusting in me to find the ways and means
Of correspondence.   Sister, rest you here.
No harm can come to you : of that be sure.
But time is precious.   Let us make this change
In our habiliments, and then one hour
For final matters and to say farewell.

ACT III.

Scene 1—THE CAVE AT PORT SODERICK. BY MOONLIGHT.

MISTRESS CHRISTIAN.

At last, my husband, to my loving heart
I clasp thee once again, and cling to thee ;
And see thy dear eyes looking into mine,
As I have seen them ever in my dreams ;
To wake and meet the cold light of the stars,
And watch until they faded far away
Into the pale gleams of the lingering dawn,
Breaking above the solemn purple hills
To usher in another dreary day.

WILLIAM CHRISTIAN.

At last, dear wife, at last. But oh ! so late.
The waiting time has been so hard to bear
That all life's joys seem frozen with despair.
I feel your warm heart beating high to mine ;
I press your gentle hand within my own ;
I clasp you to me, but with you I hold
The phantom of fair days, now past and gone,
Of Peace departed ; Hope that never more
Will light me on the the rugged paths I tread.
All seems unreal but your love, sweet wife ;
And even that may vanish into air.

MISTRESS CHRISTIAN.

No, Illiam, that will never pass away.
Friends may prove false, and fortune more unkind :
But my love waxes with the waning years,
And will be yours for ever till I die.
I know 'tis scarcely safe to venture here,

For I am watched by many curious eyes :
But oh ! I could not live another hour,
Without a word from one I love so well ;
For Sheila told me you are worn and wan,
And scarcely touch the food she brings to you.
How happy are we in this faithful friend,
Who comes and goes and passes where she will
They do not dare to watch her, in the fear
That she might cast some awful spell on them.

WILLIAM CHRISTIAN.

But at your wish I wait here.   I myself
Fear little for the Countess's revenge.
King Charles' Act of free Indemnity
Extends to this our Isle ; nor need I dread
To meet the Countess even in her wrath,
For I will live in future but for you,
Nor mix myself in party politics :
And then—

MISTRESS CHRISTIAN.

But hist !—What was that sound I heard ?

WILLIAM CHRISTIAN.

The billows, dear one, beating on the shore ;
Or the wild sea-wind moaning through the cave.

MISTRESS CHRISTIAN.

How wearily the hours must linger here,
In this vast solitude of sea and shore !
They say the mermaids haunt these gloomy caves,
And softly sing their dirges for the dead
Sleeping beneath the green depths of the sea.

WILLIAM CHRISTIAN.

But yester-eve—the tide was at the full·—
I saw a form uprising from the waves,

With milk-white breast and soft alluring eyes ;
And, as I gazed, I fancied I beheld
One of those sea-maids, whom our fisher-folk
Hold in such awe.   A moment—and it plunged,
And my sea-maiden swam away—·a seal.

MISTRESS CHRISTIAN.

Look yonder, Illiam.   Quick !—Ah ! it is gone !
Where the bright moonlight shines upon the sand,
There—where it casts the outline of the cliff—
I saw the shadow of a beckoning arm !

WILLIAM CHRISTIAN.

Your fancy, wife.   I only see some weed,
Torn from the rocks and moving in the breeze.
Be not alarmed.   There is no cause for fear :
But let us talk of fairer days to come.
The hours fly fast ; and, when the moon is high,
Sheila will come to be your escort home.
Then, but one day, and—

MISTRESS CHRISTIAN.

Hist !—I surely hear
A stealthy step.   Come more within the cave :
My ears are keen.   Now, listen.   There again !
Oh Illiam !—

CORPORAL—*enters.*

Halt, there !—And, Master Christian,
Move at your peril but a single step—
And my men fire.

MISTRESS CHRISTIAN.

Oh God !   I faint—I fall.

CORPORAL.

Yield yourself quietly, for I hold here
Warrant for your arrest.

WILLIAM CHRISTIAN.
Upon what charge ?

CORPORAL.
For treason.

WILLIAM CHRISTIAN.
Against whom ?

CORPORAL.
The Queen of Mann.

WILLIAM CHRISTIAN.
But I can claim Act of Indemnity.

CORPORAL.
Which Act does not extend so far as Mann.
I cannot waste more time in bandying words :
Submit yourself, or I make use of force.

WILLIAM CHRISTIAN.
My conscience clear, I will submit myself ;
I only ask a moment's liberty ;
For my poor wife is dying—may be dead :
See where she lies upon those cruel rocks.
I cannot leave her here in such distress.

CORPORAL.
No time have I to spare for more delay :
The woman there shall have attendance soon.
Here, Kelly ! show yourself, you skulking cur :
I leave this fainting woman in your charge,
To be accounted for by you to me.
Now, prisoner—No, not another word—
Advance, and step between the leading files.

WILLIAM CHRISTIAN.
Oh God !—One word—

CORPORAL

Obey me, sir, at once,
Unless you would be bound.　There, that will do.
Attention, soldiers!　Shoulder arms!　Quick!　March!

[*Exeunt* SOLDIERS WITH W. CHRISTIAN.]

KELLY.

Well, this has been a lucky day for me!
'Tis my turn now.　I mind me how he laughed
When I was ducked, half-drowned in Ramsay Bay.
'Twas well I kept my eye on that old witch,
Who passes to and fro from Ronaldsway.
Attend to Christian's wife?—Yes; I'll attend!
But first to see if they are well away.—
No, not a sound except the lapping tide.—
So now, my lady, to attend to you.
First for your pockets: papers—keys—a book.
And what is this?—Good luck!　A purse of gold!
What!　Waking up?—Ah!　That will never do.
I'll tie this bit of twine—but not too tight—
Around your slender throat; and, if you move,
Why you may never wake on earth again.
Now for your ring.　So small—I pull and pull—
I'll have it though.　Confound it, how it clings!

SHEILA CRANE—*enters—cautiously.*

Ah!　What is there stretched out upon the rocks?
Fair Mistress Christian?　No.　It cannot be;
And yet 'tis she.　And kneeling by her side—
I'll creep a little closer—Treachery!—
That villain, Kelly Dhoo!—Strike, trusty steel,
And strike him deep and sure.　Take that—and that!

MISTRESS CHRISTIAN—*faintly—*

Oh!　Illiam—Illiam come!—This fearful dream!
Where are you, Illiam dear?　Oh!　answer me!

What, Sheila ?—Ah ! I wake.   Those cruel men—
Oh, Sheila ! weave your spells upon their path,
And stay their steps.   They've taken him away :
They've dragged him even from my circling arms !—
I had no power to hold him.   He is gone.
Ah, God !—What's this ?   They've slain him at my side.
Oh let me raise him—press him to my heart—
And bring him back to love and life once more !

SHEILA.

Sweet mistress, come with me.   He is not there.
Defile not your fair feet with that black stream.
There lies the traitor who has wrought this ill—
Struck down by Sheila's arm.   There let him lie—
To welter in his gore until the tide,
Returning, bear the carrion away.
Rise up.—Rise up at once, and come with me,¯
Your faithful Sheila ; for our Illiam lives,
And we will try to save him.   Come, dear, come !

Scene 2.—CASTLE RUSHEN.   ATTENDANT *enters*.

ATTENDANT.

A lady, madam, closely veiled is here,
And asks for audience.

COUNTESS OF DERBY.

What may be her name ?

ATTENDANT.

She seemed averse to let me know her name.

COUNTESS OF DERBY.

Then she must go unheard.   I cannot grant
An interview to every nameless trull
Who seeks my presence.   Bid her go her way.

ATTENDANT.

I think her voice, though almost choked with sobs,
Was Mistress Christian's.

COUNTESS OF DERBY.
What ! That woman here ?
Then I will see her. Bring her here at once.
Now shall I sip the sweets of my revenge—(*aside*).

MISTRESS CHRISTIAN—*enters*.
Madam, I come to you ; I cry to you ;
And even on my knees do I implore
That you will grant me mercy. I have come
No more to plead in virtue of his cause,
No more to cavil at injustice done,
No more presuming on indemnity ;
But as a woman, at a woman's feet,
I beg of you to spare my husband's life.
Imprison me—with torture if you will,
Or let my life be forfeited for his :
But, as a woman, show a woman's heart,
And let me see some pity in your eyes.
Bend down, I pray thee, from thy place of power,
And stretch between him and the keen-edged blade,
Which Justice wields sometimes so cruelly,
The silvern shield of Mercy. Spare his life,
And give my husband back again to me.

COUNTESS OF DERBY.
Thy husband, Mistress Christian ? Where is mine·
How dare you even whisper such a name
In this my presence ? Justice shall be done ;
But, as for Mercy, she took wing and fled
When I, a prisoner in these very walls—
Betrayed by him for whom you come to plead—
Lay chafing out my heart those weary years.
Mercy, forsooth ! I know not such a name.

MISTRESS CHRISTIAN.

Madam, my husband never injured thee,
When he gave up the Isle to Cromwell's arms.
He acted on compulsion ; and for thee
I know he pleaded honestly and well
You might have lived in honour anywhere,
But that you marred your cause with bitter words.
Oh ! madam, pass such memories away,
And grant the grace I crave—my husband's life

COUNTESS OF DERBY.

Considering your place and circumstance,
You speak bold words.

MISTRESS CHRISTIAN.
Madam, the puny wren
Would ruffle out her plumes, in hope to save
Her wounded mate from danger.   Grace, I pray.

COUNTESS OF DERBY.

I have no grace to grant.   So plead no more.
All grace departed when great Stanley died.

MISTRESS CHRISTIAN.

Grant him, I pray thee, but a few more days ;
Reprieve will come ere long from England's King,
Who surely would not sanction or allow
Such cruel murder.

COUNTESS OF DERBY.
No—I tell you—No.
He dies to-morrow morn.   Had I my will,
So far from sparing such a treacherous knave,
I would invent some ignominious death,
To match his treason.   Had he forty lives,
He should die forty deaths ; and every death
Should bear a different torture in its train.

6

MISTRESS CHRISTIAN.

Ah ! It is horrible to hear such words.
Have you no pity left within your breast ?
Grant but one week—his pardon must arrive—
And do not stain your hands with guiltless blood.

COUNTESS OF DERBY.

I tell you No, Dame Christian. He must die
To-morrow morn at day-break. I have said.

MISTRESS CHRISTIAN.

Grant me at least to see him ere he die ;
And with me Sheila Craine, who waits me here.

COUNTESS OF DERBY.

What ! That vile witch ? She shall not enter here,
To bring a potion, or to weave a spell
To rescue him from his just punishment.
Go tell her I have marked her conduct well,
And that, ere long, imprisoned she shall roll
Within a well-spiked barrel to her doom,
Down steep Slieu Whallin. Tell her this from me.

MISTRESS CHRISTIAN.

Oh ! Madam, pity us.

COUNTESS OF DERBY.
Pity, forsooth !
I do not know the meaning of the word.
At dawn to-morrow be at Hango Hill,
And listen till a roll of musketry
Shall warn the people of a traitor's doom.
Then you may see your husband if you will,
But not before. Now, Mistress Christian,—go.

Scene 3.—THE STONE CIRCLE AT BALLAMONA.

SHEILA CRAINE.

There's shelter here, dear Mistress. Rest awhile
Behind these time-worn stones. Your weary feet
Are bruised and bleeding, and your silken robe
Is drenched and clinging round you with the rain.

MISTRESS CHRISTIAN.

'Tis little matter what befalls me now ;
For all my life went out from me to-day
With his pure spirit. Never—never more
Shall I feel joy or sorrow, peace or pain :
My heart is dead within me, and my blood
Is chilled within my veins. Ah direful day !
My very tears have left my eyelids dry,
And I can weep no more. Oh cruel day
That drew my dear one from my life away !
Weep for him, clouds, and pour your grief in rain ;
Wail for him, winds, with all your wild despair ;
The noblest truest man has passed away
That ever breathed God's air.—So foully slain !

SHEILA CRAINE.

Didst mark that fiery meteor cross the sky,
Where the clouds bank and hover o'er the hills ?
Perchance his spirit ranging through the air,
In search for vengeance on his enemies !

MISTRESS CHRISTIAN.

Nay, Sheila. Rather there his spirit flies
Where yon fair star is breaking through the gloom.
Beneficent and beautiful its beams
Shine down upon us through a mist of tears.
He was too brave—too true, to seek revenge.
He loved our people, and he gave his life
To win them liberty—and he is dead—

6A

And they are living to enjoy their gains—
And I am left alone—to weep my loss.

SHEILA CRAINE.

My curses light on them, the cowardly curs—
Upon their homes, their cattle and their grain !
May all they eat turn bitter in their maws !
Sleeping or waking may they know no rest,
But die like rotten sheep upon the hills—
Food for the ravens and the carrion crows !
When he went out so bravely to his doom,
Where were ye then, ye manly men of Mann?
In stern array to wrest him from Death's grasp ?
Or crouching 'neath the roof-trees of those homes
Which he won for you, even with his life?
What were ye doing when he wanted aid ?
Shedding pale tears instead of your red blood !
Did any ever ask *his* aid in vain ?
My curse upon ye, manly men of Mann !
Not one of ye was worth his finger's tip.
My curse upon ye for all time to be,
And may dire judgment seize upon——

MISTRESS CHRISTIAN.*
Oh, cease,
Dear Sheila, cease such bitter words, I pray.

SHEILA CRAINE *continues.*

No more shall old Phynodderee's hairy limbs
Toil for ye and bring fortune to your fields ;
No more shall fay be with ye.   But again
The Goths shall come in all their foul array,
Defiling sacred cross and runic stone,
Driving their smoking steeds from glen to glen,

---

* The following lines may be omitted, continuing at Edward Christian's
' What now ? "

And scattering ye beneath their chariot wheels,
Till all the Island shall be over-run;
Fair Douglas Town a mixen for their hordes,
And Kelly's name held in such high disdain
That every child shall yell it through the Isle
In execration. And on England's shore
Alike my curse shall fall. From yon green Isle,
Far in the west, I hear a windy cry
Swelling across the sea for Liberty.
I see a grim grey chief, a verbose man,
Uplifting a fell axe and hewing down
The pillars of the State like forest trees.
I see the serfs in countless myriads rise,
Hear them out-talk their rulers, and demand
For every hind three acres and——

EDWARD CHRISTIAN—*enters*.
                    What now?
Speak, or I fire! Who lurks behind those stones?
Come forth, foul spies, and face me if ye dare.

MISTRESS CHRISTIAN.
Two lonely women resting on their way—
No spies are we.

EDWARD CHRISTIAN.
                    That voice! What! Sheltering here,
Poor sister, from the storm? And Sheila, too?
Thank God that I have found you. Do not fear:
'Tis only I, his brother, wandering—
With soul on fire and burning for revenge
Upon this dastard deed.

MISTRESS CHRISTIAN.
                    Oh! Edward, say,
And were you present when they slew my love?

EDWARD CHRISTIAN.
Dear sister, in disguise I waited near,
In hope to rouse the people ; but I failed.
They would not even strike a single blow,
Although they might have saved him had they dared :
But every arm was paralysed by fear.
When he came forth—

MISTRESS CHRISTIAN.
Ah ! tell me how he died.

EDWARD CHRISTIAN.
Boldly and bravely as an honest man.
When he had passed, well guarded, through the crowd,
He stood awhile as though in earnest thought ;
And then he raised his hand and spake these.words :
'Mourn not for me, my people, that I die,
For I stand innocent of any crime
Against the Countess and my loyalty.
Unjustly tried, I meet my death to-day
In patience ; freely offering myself
In sacrifice for those I love so well.
So be ye patient too, but hold my name,
When I am gone, in kindly memory ;
And think of me as one who did not fear
To give his life to gain you liberty.
Mourn not for me, for I shall be at rest.
Of late my days have passed in misery.
Knowing no place where I might lay my head :
But now, secure in God's forgiving grace,
All persecution will be passed away.
So I at last may find the peace I crave,
For though He kill me—yet I trust in Him.
Let there be no more risings in the Isle ;
But act as loyal lieges, and obey
Your rulers in all just commands, and be
Loyal to one another in your homes.

What I have said and proved in my defence
To show my guiltlessness, they may suppress ;
But ye who know me know I do not lie,
And I assert that I am innocent.
Farewell, my people ! May God's blessing light
Upon you and your homes ! May He forgive
Those who have injured me and wrought my doom,
As I forgive them !'

MISTRESS CHRISTIAN.
Oh ! my Illiam,
What could possess them so to injure thee?

EDWARD CHRISTIAN.
Then, sister, then he fell upon his knees,
And asked the prayers of all who stood around,
And wrapped himself in prayer.   Then, rising up,
He smiled and, looking where the soldiers stood,
Addressed them thus : 'Now to your duty, men,
Appointed and allotted out to you.
I blame you not.   The only boon I ask
Is that you place no bandage on my eyes,
But let me stand here, free, to face your fire,
And meet your bullets as becomes a man.'

MISTRESS CHRISTIAN.
Oh ! How could they have had the heart to fire?

EDWARD CHRISTIAN.
Then, pinning a white favour to his breast,
He spake to them again.   'Strike, soldiers, here ;
And do, at my command, your work and mine.
Let no hand falter.   Fear not I shall quail.
Now, soldiers, ready !   Take fair aim—and—Fire !'
And, as he fell, a mighty sob went out
From all the people—'Illiam Dhône is dead !'
Bear up, poor sister.   He was brave and true.

Henceforward you shall ever be my care;
And we will fly this Island to some home
Where you and yours may rest in peace at last :
And Sheila, too, shall pass away with us—

SHEILA CRAINE.

No, Edward Christian, I will wait me here,
So that, when I have lived my lotted span,
My spirit may go forth and linger here,
To teach the birds to carol Illiam Dhône;
The waving woods to whisper Illiam Dhône :
The rippling streams to murmur Illiam Dhône;
The mighty sea to thunder Illiam Dhône;—
Till all the Isle shall echo with his name,
To tingle in men's ears and haunt their hearts
For ever with the memory of his wrongs.

EDWARD CHRISTIAN.

And I, too, have a mission to fulfil,
Nor shall I rest till I accomplish it.
Mine be it to avenge my brother's death,
And show no mercy to his murderers.

MISTRESS CHRISTIAN.

And mine to mourn him till my days be done.

www.ingramcontent.com/pod-product-compliance
Lightning Source LLC
Chambersburg PA
CBHW030906260626
47169CB00008B/2707